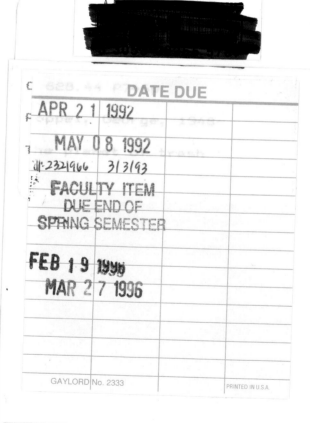

the Planet of Trash

by George Poppel

Illustrated by Barry Moyer

National Press, Inc.
7508 Wiconsin Avenue
Bethesda, Maryland 20814

(301) 657-1616

The Planet of Trash
by George Poppel
Illustrated by Barry Moyer
© National Press, Inc. 1987
7508 Wisconsin Avenue
Bethesda, Maryland 20814
(301) 657-1616

Library of Congress Cataloging-in-Publication Data
Poppel, George, 1948-
    The planet of trash.
    (Panda monium books)
    Summary: Describes in rhyme what astronauts from
outer space discover when they land on the planet
"Trash" in the year 2052 and discusses ways that people
can keep the earth clean.
    1. Refuse and refuse disposal – Juvenile literature.
2. Pollution – Environmental aspects – Juvenile literature.
3. Man – Influence on nature – Juvenile literature.
4. Picture – books for children. [1. Refuse and refuse
disposal. 2. Pollution. 3. Man – Influence on natural]
I. Moyer, Barry, ill.   II. Title.
TD792.P67   1987   628.4'4   87-5741

ISBN 0-915765-42-X
ISBN 0-915765-46-X (pbk.)

Dedication

This book is dedicated
to the future generations
of the Planet Earth.

the Planet of Trash

It was in the year 2,052,
in a place that we knew.
Astronauts from outer space,
descendants of a different race,
landed on the planet "Trash"
covered up in blackened ash.

They came from the planet Artemis
and arrived amid char and mist
on a mission to discover,
unearth, detect or uncover
what had happened to the Planet of Trash:
Did it explode? Or did it crash?

The astronaut's mission at hand
was to bring back samples of land.
And to preserve remnants of air,
which scientists would compare
with the clean atmosphere of home,
where they had left their families alone.

They dug into the filthy ground
until they heard a crunching sound.
They had hit an old tin can,
a rusty wheel, a frying pan,
a plastic fork, an old armchair—
Maybe someone once lived there!

The extraterrestrial explorers
roamed the planet on orders.
They bored holes
and discovered coals.
Then they made the biggest find:
Cola bottles were there to be mined!

Near the cola bottle lodes
they found highways and roads.
And crashed heaps of cars,
coated with dirt and with tar.
They called it the "Cola Car Pits."
And the name certainly fits.

Their scientists derived a theory
to explain the unusual debris:
Cola was a dirty fuel
made of toxic molecules,
and cars were powered by cola beans:
That explained the soda machines!

Cola beans were a dirty fuel source.
They produced black fumes, of course.
Which explains the blackened air:
Didn't anybody seem to care?

The cola smoke made the planet too hot.
Few plants could live, most could not.
When the plants wilted and turned brown
no one lived to stay around.
They had killed themselves with pollution:
Wasn't there a better solution?

I did not intend to scare
you about breathing dirty air.
But the Planet of Trash could be the Planet Earth.
How much is a clean planet worth?
Do we value clean air and water
as much as we ought to?

This book is not a true story
but you still have reason to worry.
Because people are treating our planet like junk,
by dumping garbage, plastic and gunk
into our playgrounds, fields and lakes.
Stop them from making these awful mistakes.

You can help too—it's not so rough.
Pick up your toys and trash and stuff.
Keep our planet Earth clean and make it better,
recycle things and do not litter.
Being ecological won't give you a rash!
Do you want to live on a planet of trash?

The
End

Ordering Information

Panda Monium Books are published by the National Press, Inc. To order copies of the following books send a check or money order payable to the National Press, Inc. Add $1.25 per book for postage and handling. Maryland residents add 5% for sales tax. Master and Visa credit cards are accepted. Order by phone, toll-free (800) NA-BOOKS.

Title	Price
The Planet of Trash	$ 9.95
The Magic Word (Hardcover)	$ 9.95
Au Pair American Style	$ 5.95
Good Toys: Parents Guide to Toys and Games	$ 5.95
Father/Son Book (Hardcover)	$12.95
Father/Son Book (Paperback)	$5.95